Truck, Truck, GOOSE!

Story by **Tammi Sauer**   Pictures by **Zoe Waring**

HARPER
An Imprint of HarperCollinsPublishers

Picnic To-Do List: ✩
✩ Choose picnic spot. ☑
Pack a big lunch. ☑
Take _everything_ I need. ☐

HarperCollins

Truck, Truck, Goose!
Text copyright © 2017 by Tammi Sauer
Illustrations copyright © 2017 by Zoe Waring
All rights reserved. Manufactured in China.
No part of this book may be used or reproduced in any manner whatsoever without written permission except in the case of brief quotations embodied in critical articles and reviews. For information address HarperCollins Children's Books, a division of HarperCollins Publishers, 195 Broadway, New York, NY 10007.
www.harpercollinschildrens.com

ISBN 978-0-06-242153-1

The artist used digital brushes to create the illustrations for this book.
Typography by Rachel Zegar
17 18 19 20 21 SCP 10 9 8 7 6 5 4 3 2 1

◆
First Edition

For Pierce—who is always on the move
—T.S.

To my husband—for fueling my imagination
with fun and laughter each day
—Z.W.

Truck…

Truck...

Truck...

Truck...

Truck...

Truck...

Goose.

Truck...

Truck...

Truck...

FISH

Goose.

Truck...

Truck...

Truck...

Truck...

Pie
"Mmmmmmm!"

Goose.

MOOSE!